A Christmas Musical for Choir

GLORIOUS Joy!

BY O. D. HALL JR.

Lillenas
PUBLISHING COMPANY
Kansas City, MO 64141

CONTENTS

The Angels' Celebration

Angels We Have Heard on High
Hark! the Herald Angels Sing
Angels, from the Realms of Glory
The Birthday of a King

Arranged by O. D. Hall, Jr.

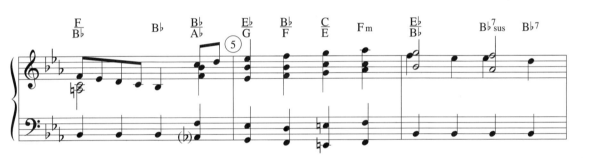

"Angels We Have Heard on High"
1st time: Choir
2nd time: Ladies

1. An - gels we have
2. Come to Beth - le -

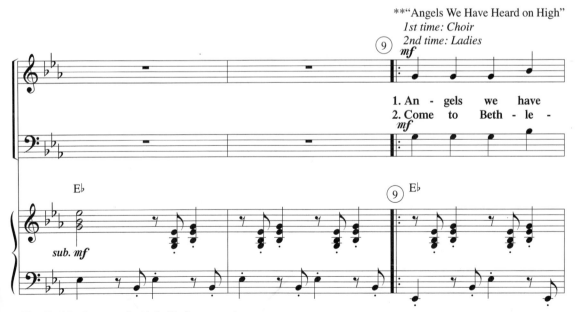

*Note: Track has 1 measure of cymbal roll before measure 1

*"Hark! the Herald Angels Sing"

*"Angels, from the Realms of Glory"

12

It was the birth-day of Je - sus, Sing glo - - - ri - a! Wor - ship Je - sus Christ, the new - born King!

Carols Sing

PAUL and MARTHA PUCKETT

MARTHA PUCKETT
Arranged by O. D. Hall, Jr.

PLEASE NOTE: Copying of this product is not covered by CCLI licenses. For CCLI information call 1-800-234-2446.

While Shepherds Watched

Underscore

GEORGE FREDERICK HANDEL
Arranged by O. D. Hall, Jr.
*Narrator begins

*NARRATOR: There were shepherds living out in the fields near Bethlehem, keeping watch over their flocks at night. An Angel of the Lord appeared to them, and the glory

of the Lord shone around them, and they were terrified. But the angel said to them, "Do not be afraid. I bring you good news of great joy that will be for all the people.

Today in the town of David a Savior has been born to you; He is Christ the Lord. This will be a sign to you; You will find a baby wrapped in strips of cloth and lying in a manger."

Suddenly a great company of the heavenly host appeared with the angel, praising God and saying, "Glory to God in the highest, and on earth peace to men on whom His favor rests." *(Luke 2:8-14)*

And Glory Shone Around

NAHUM TATE and
O. D. HALL, JR.

O. D. HALL, JR.
Arranged by O. D. Hall, Jr.

Beautiful Name
Underscore

MABEL JOHNSTON CAMP
Arranged by O. D. Hall, Jr.

NARRATOR: *(without music)* This is how the birth of Jesus Christ came about. *(music begins)* His mother Mary was pledged to be married to Joseph, but before they came

together, she was found to be with child through the Holy Spirit. Because Joseph her husband was a righteous man and did not want to expose her to public disgrace, He had

in mind to divorce her quietly. But after he had considered this, an angel of the Lord appeared to him in a dream and said, "Joseph, son of David, do not be afraid to take

Mary home as your wife, because what is conceived in her is from the Holy Spirit. She will give birth to a Son, and you are to give Him the name Jesus, because He will save His people from their sins." *(Matthew 1:18-21)*

Jesus Is His Name

Words and Music by
STEVE AMERSON
and O. D. HALL, JR.
Arranged by O. D. Hall, Jr.

And the an-gels sang, "Glo - ry to God,"___ And the shep-herds sang,

Speak His Name

Words and Music by
MOSIE LISTER
Arranged by O. D. Hall, Jr.

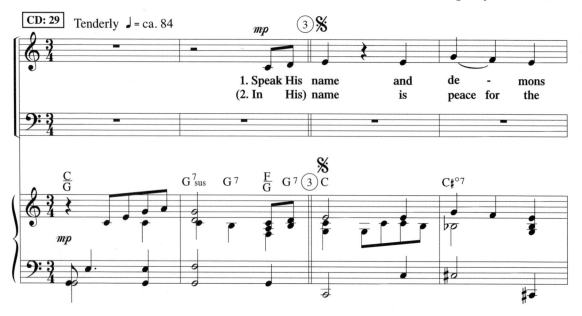

1. Speak His name and de - mons
(2. In His) name is peace for the

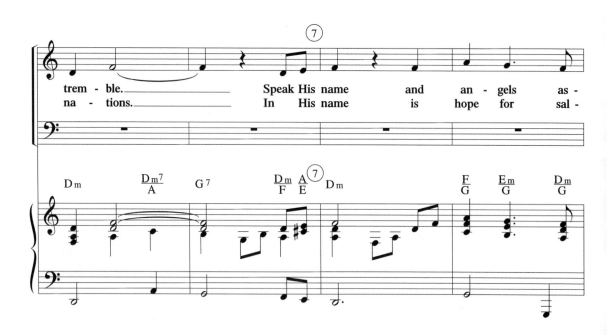

trem - ble.___ Speak His name and an - gels as -
na - tions.___ In His name is hope for sal -

42

In a Manger

Underscore

O. D. HALL, JR.

*NARRATOR: When the angels had left them and gone into heaven, the shepherds said

*Narrator begins

to one another, "Let's go to Bethlehem and see this thing that has happened, which the Lord has told us about."

So they hurried off and found Mary and Joseph, and the baby, who was lying in the manger. When they had seen Him, they spread the word concerning what had been told

them about this child, and all who heard it were amazed at what the shepherds said to them. *Luke 2:15-18)*

Good News!

with
Joy to the World

Words and Music by
MARTY PARKS
Arranged by O. D. Hall, Jr.

sud - den - ly were daz - zled by a blind - ing light;

Choir
Good news!__ Good news!

Solo (Optional men)
Well, the an - gel of the Lord God ap -

peared to them,__ Good news!__ Good news!

Choir

Solo (Optional men)
Said the

CD: 35

Savior had been born down in Beth - le - hem.

Good news! Good news! Good news of

our sal - va - tion, Good news for ev - ery na - tion;

50

Come, O Come, Emmanuel
Underscore

O. D. HALL, JR.

*NARRATOR: Come, O come, Emmanuel.

To our disenchanted world be our Wonderful Counselor;

To our weak and powerless lives be our Mighty God;

To our fragmented families be our Everlasting Father;

To our strained and shattered relationships be our Prince of Peace.

O come, Emmanuel…from Your glory to our world; from Your eternity to our lives;
from Your throne to our hearts.

A Stable Prayer

KEN BIBLE

TOM FETTKE
Arranged by O. D. Hall, Jr.

We Bow Down

Words and Music by
TWILA PARIS
Arranged by O. D. Hall, Jr.

King of all kings You will be. King of all kings

You will be!

Worship the Sovereign Lord

Sovereign Lord
All Hail the Power of Jesus' Name
A Stable Prayer

Arranged by O. D. Hall, Jr.

*NARRATOR: At the name of Jesus every knee should bow, and every tongue confess that Jesus Christ is Lord.

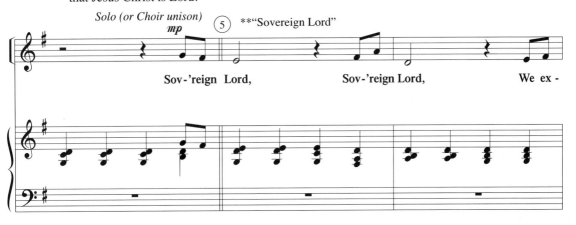

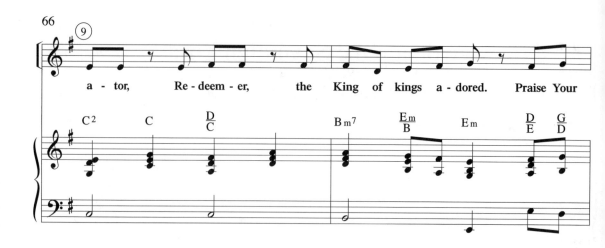

CD: 48

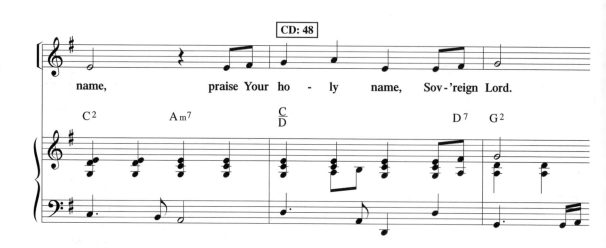

68

*"All Hail the Power of Jesus' Name"

70

72

Finale

Carols Sing
And Glory Shone Around
Jesus Is His Name
Good News!
Joy to the World

Arranged by O. D. Hall, Jr.

*Note: Track has 1 measure of cymbal roll before measure 1

**Words by Paul and Martha Puckett; Music by Martha Puckett. © Copyright 1990 Broadman Press. All rights reserved. Used by permission.

*"Jesus Is His Name"

*"Joy to the World"

Go tell the world the glo- r'ous word– That Christ the Lord is here. Let tid - ings___ of___ great joy___ be heard___ Re - sound-ing loud and__ clear, Re - sound-ing loud and__ clear, Go___

Jesus Is His Name

Words and Music by
STEVE AMERSON and
O. D. HALL, JR.

1. Love has come to Beth-le-hem, Je-sus is His name.
2. Love has come to us to-day, Je-sus is His name.

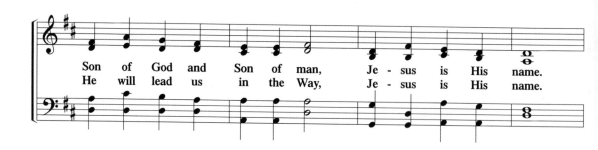

Son of God and Son of man, Je-sus is His name.
He will lead us in the Way, Je-sus is His name.

Un-to us a Child has come,___ He was born to reign;___
Un-to us the Lord has come___ In our hearts to reign;___

God's re-demp-tion in His Son, Je-sus is His name.
God's re-demp-tion in His Son, Je-sus is His name.

GLORIOUS Joy!

GLORIOUS
Joy!

GLORIOUS
Joy!

GLORIOUS
Joy!

GLORIOUS
Joy!

GLORIOUS
Joy!